CRIMSON TWILL

WITCH IN THE CITY

CRIMSON TWILL

TWILL

WITCH IN THE CITY

KALLIE GEORGE

illustrated by BIRGITTA SIF

CANDLEWICK PRESS

Text copyright © 2022 by Kallie George
Illustrations copyright © 2022 by Birgitta Sif

First edition 2022

Library of Congress Catalog Card Number 2021947903
ISBN 978-1-5362-1463-5

22 23 24 25 26 27 LBM 10 9 8 7 6 5 4 3 2 1

Printed in Melrose Park, IL, USA

This book was typeset in Garamond.
The illustrations were created digitally.

Candlewick Press
99 Dover Street
Somerville, Massachusetts 02144

www.candlewick.com

FSC
www.fsc.org

MIX
From responsible
sources
FSC® C103098

To Luke, for that moment when you said,
"Witch City!"

KG

To brave and unique girls everywhere,
the world needs you!

BS

TABLE OF CONTENTS

1

CRIMSON TWILL

Crimson Twill was a little witch. But you might not know it. She didn't look like a typical little witch. Instead of wearing pointy shoes, she wore gum boots. Instead of wearing a plain black dress, she wore a polka-dotted one. And instead of wearing a plain black hat, she wore one with a big bow, and the hat was crimson, just like her name.

Crimson didn't act like a typical little witch, either. She giggled instead of cackled. She skipped instead of slunk around. And instead of having nightmares, like witches were supposed to, Crimson *dreamed*.

Tonight was a dream come true.

It was Crimson's first trip to Broomingdale's.

Crimson lived in Cackle County, in a cottage with her mom. She loved it there—the fields of broom straw, the deep dark woods, and the bats in their barn. Still, sometimes Cackle County was lonely for a little witch. Crimson was thrilled to be going to the city. And especially to Broomingdale's. It was bound to be full of exciting new things. Not like the Cackle Country Store, which was so dreary and dusty, it even sold dust.

She had been to New Wart City only twice before. Once to visit her Aunt Mildew, who worked at the Spell Book Publishing House. (That was fun because she got to meet her favorite ghost writer.) Another time to visit the Museum of Magical Art on a school field trip. (That wasn't fun because their tour guide was a grumpy ogre.)

But she had never been shopping at Broomingdale's. It was the biggest department store in the world. It opened when the stars shone. Witches flew in from all corners of the country to shop there. Her mom went only once in a blue moon. And this time, she had decided Crimson was old enough to join her.

Best of all, Crimson had some money to spend. Five gold coins!

She had earned them. She had worked hard cleaning the cauldron after supper, feeding the frogs in the pond, and sweeping the bridge for the troll next door. She didn't tell her mom that she had gotten the broom to do all the sweeping for her. But wasn't that what the cleaning broom was for?

Now the coins jingled in her pocket as she and her mom flew down to the Speedy Underground Broomway.

What should I buy? Crimson wondered.

Maybe a new wand. Full-length instead of half-size. But was she really ready for a full-length wand?

Maybe a new dress. But she liked her polka-dotted dress, with its spider-shaped buttons. Nobody else had one like it. Granny Twill had conjured it just for her. "Unique like you," cackled Granny. Granny Twill was a really good spellstress.

Maybe some new shoes. But her gum boots still fit. And they were charmed to make extra-big splashes in mud puddles.

I'll find something special when we get there, she decided.

Maybe there were things at Broomingdale's Crimson couldn't even dream up. And she was good at dreaming.

Which was useful now, because the Speedy Underground Broomway wasn't very speedy. "We should have taken the Upper Broomway," sighed her mom. "It's always impossible to know which will be worse."

In front and behind them stretched a long line of brooms and somber, stylish witches. Only Crimson was dressed differently.

Ads flashed on the tunnel walls as they passed.

"Crooked Combs—For Split Ends and Endless Knots!"

"Cauldron Cola—Guaranteed to Rot Your Teeth!"

"The Terribly Tasteful Triplets star in *Which Witch Is Which?*"

A wizard with a tray swooped around the slow-moving traffic. "Late for a meeting? Get a disgustingly delicious deli sandwich!" he called. "Have some flies on the fly!"

A giant toad three brooms ahead ordered four. *Croak!* "Yum!"

At last, traffic picked up, and Crimson and her mom came to a blinking sign: EXIT, NEW WART CENTRAL PARK.

"Not that one," her mom said and kept flying.

EXIT, SLIME SQUARE.

"Not that one, either."

Then up ahead, Crimson saw EXIT, 13TH AVENUE.

"That's it," said her mom, pulling up sharply. Good thing Crimson was holding on with a tight grip!

Up, up, up they flew through the exit and into the sky.

They had been flying for a *very* long time. When they had started out, the sky was bright. Now it was dusky. The stars were beginning to twinkle.

Or were those stars?

Crimson blinked.

No! They weren't. They were the lights of New Wart City.

And, above the lights, a silver, moon-shaped sign flashed:

At last, they had made it!

2

BROOMINGDALE'S

Bugs and bones, it's busy," moaned Crimson's mom, gazing around Broomingdale's roof. "I forgot it was the night of the fashion show." Every single space on every single parking rack bore a broom.

"Can you see any free spots?" she asked Crimson.

Crimson spied a witch heading out, her broom loaded down with bags. "There's one!"

Another witch tried to swoop in, but Crimson's mom swooped faster. They snatched the spot—just in time.

"Wow!" said Crimson.

"You have to be zippy when you're in the city," her mom replied.

Crimson slid off the back of the broom. Her mom leaned the broom between the bars on the rack and waved her wand:

Hicky picky, lock and stay.
A witch who touches soon will pay.

Crimson had never heard this spell before. In the country, they left their brooms leaning against the door.

"I'd better check my list," said her mom.

She pulled a scroll out of her pocket. It unrolled down to the ground.

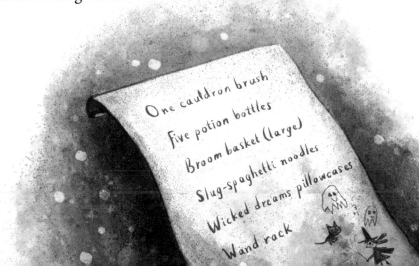

One cauldron brush
Five potion bottles
Broom basket (large)
Slug-spaghetti noodles
Wicked dreams pillowcases
Wand rack

As her mom read on and on, Crimson glanced at two city witchlings passing by.

"Rats and bats! We have to miss all the fun," said one. "Only our troll of a teacher would assign an enchantment essay due the *same* night as Broomingdale's big fashion show!"

"And Vera Fang's capes are cutting edge," added the other.

"Hi!" said Crimson.

The teen witchlings didn't reply.

Instead, they sniffed at her dress. Then they walked away, toward their brooms.

Crimson told herself to ignore them. She liked her cheery dress.

She turned back to her mom.

"We'll start on the Cauldron floor," said her mom as she rolled up her list and put it back in her pocket. "Then we'll head to Potion Accessories."

"What about me?" asked Crimson. "I don't want a cauldron. Or any potions."

Her mom thought for a moment. "Very well," she said. "You can meet me at the Moonlight Café at midnight. It's just over there."

Underneath the Broomingdale's sign, on the roof, was a restaurant. Through the enormous windows, Crimson could see that it was filled with glittering chairs and tables. And lots and lots of witches!

"It must be very popular," said Crimson.

"They are famous for their pie," said her mom.

Crimson loved frog-eye pie. Her stomach rumbled. But she was here to shop, not eat.

"If you need me, just wave your wand and I'll be there in a twinkling," said her mom. "Now, come on. This way to the elevator."

Crimson hurried after her.

Ding! The elevator doors opened. Out spilled witches all dressed the same, carrying small, medium, and big shopping bags and reeking of bug's breath perfume.

Crimson plugged her nose—no one wore bug's breath perfume in Cackle County—and she and her mom stepped inside. Her mom pressed a button shaped like a cauldron.

Which one should I press? thought Crimson.

There were so many to choose from: a broom-shaped button, a hat-shaped button, even a button shaped like a wart. "For permanent wart placements," explained her mom. "But don't even think about it. Stick-ons are still fine for you."

Crimson rolled her eyes. Secretly, though, she was

happy with stick-ons. A permanent wart sounded like it might hurt!

She decided to press the button shaped like a cat. She loved cats. Maybe that's what she should get.

A pet cat *would* keep her company. And maybe Broomingdale's had a cat that liked to cuddle and curl up on your lap instead of hiss and help with hexes. What a great friend that would be.

Or maybe she could even find a puppy. She'd heard of puppies, but she'd never seen one. Most witches preferred cats because they were good at balancing on brooms. But Crimson imagined a little puppy snuggled in a basket on the back of hers when she learned to ride. Wouldn't *that* be fun!

She pressed the button.

"Ooooh! Not so hard, not so hard!" said the elevator.

Down, down, down went the elevator.

Then . . . *Ding!* The button shaped like a cat lit up. The elevator doors opened.

"Remember, meet me at the café in one hour," said her mom. "And if you need me—"

"Just wave my wand," finished Crimson. "I'll be fine, Mom."

Crimson wriggled past two other witches. Truth be told, she was a little nervous. But mostly, she was excited! Then, with a goodbye to her mom, she skipped out onto the Cat floor.

3

THE CAT FLOOR

Purring, hissing, scratching, licking. Hundreds of cats filled the Cat floor. The cats weren't in cages but on cushions, on row after row of shelves. Below each cat was a sign with its name and price. None of them seemed particularly cuddly or even extra-magical. But Crimson could imagine . . .

"Thunder" sounded as big as a pumpkin, with rumbling snores and lightning spiking from his tail. "Cleo" sounded regal and tall, a cat fit for a witchy queen. And "Moonbeam"—Crimson smiled to herself—would glow like the moon, like the broom straw fields on her farm.

She sighed. But that was just her imagination. These cats were no different from the ones at home.

That reminded her. Granny Twill's barn cat was going to have kittens soon. Granny Twill had said that she could have one. Crimson didn't need a cat, after all.

She was about to move on to a different floor when she heard a strange, soft whimper.

It was coming from down by her feet. There, underneath a shelf, crouched a tiny animal. It had ears and a tail and a nose like a cat. But it didn't look like a cat. It didn't have a sign. But it did have a collar.

Crimson crouched down, too.

She read its collar: PEPPER.

Pepper looked at her. His tail trembled, and he made his funny noise again. This time it was extra-sad sounding.

"It's okay," Crimson said. She reached out and carefully scooped him up.

Crimson looked this way and that. Finally, she saw a saleswitch at the back, wearing a Broomingdale's cloak with the letter *B* on it. The saleswitch was gazing at herself in a floating mirror and brushing her shiny black hair. Over and over again. She had a small nose and long nails. She looked just like a cat.

"Excuse me," said Crimson brightly.

The saleswitch twitched her nose but didn't answer.

"Excuse me," Crimson repeated.

"Go away," purred the saleswitch. "Can't you see I'm busy?"

"But . . ." Wasn't it the job of a saleswitch to help a customer? "I'd like to buy this pet, please."

The saleswitch turned. Her tag read MS. WHISKERS.

"He was under a shelf," said Crimson. "His name is Pepper."

Ms. Whiskers peered at Crimson's dress and then at Pepper. Her nose twitched again. "You cannot buy that pet. That is not one of *our* cats," she hissed. *"That . . ."* She stared at Pepper's wagging tail. "Is a puppy!"

So this was a puppy! Puppies *were* really cute, just like she imagined.

But Ms. Whiskers didn't seem to think so.

"Only cats are sold at Broomingdale's. Someone must have smuggled him in here. But he cannot stay. I can get rid of him with a Dog-Gone spell."

"Oh, please, no!" said Crimson. She clutched Pepper. "I'll look after him."

"Certainly not. Dogs are *not* allowed in Broomingdale's," said Ms. Whiskers, reaching into her cloak.

Crimson thought fast. She took out her wand. But she didn't cast a spell. She pointed. "Is that a mouse?" she said, gesturing under the mirror.

"A mouse!" exclaimed Ms. Whiskers.

As Ms. Whiskers crouched to look, Crimson slipped away.

"I'll keep you for now," said Crimson to Pepper. "Until we find your owner."

She picked up a shopping basket and put Pepper in

it. He wiggled and made another strange sound again. *Ruff! Ruff!*

"Shhh. You have to stay hidden for now," said Crimson.

Pepper seemed to understand. He curled up and wagged his tail. He looked happy.

Which made Crimson feel happy, too, even if she hadn't found anything yet to buy.

4

THE BROOM FLOOR

Back in the elevator, Crimson pressed the button shaped like a broom. This time very lightly.

"Hehehe, that tickles!" giggled the elevator.

Crimson couldn't wait to fly her own broom, but she wasn't quite old enough. She often imagined all the fun she'd have when she was. She wasn't going to fly in a straight line. No. She was going to do swoops and spirals and spine-tingling spins. Just like Ms. Trix, the famous stunt flier. Ms. Trix had even flown over a rainbow. Crimson dreamed of doing that. Maybe she could find a book on stunts so she could study ahead.

Down, down, down went the elevator.

Ding! The button shaped like a broom lit up. The elevator doors opened.

As soon as Crimson stepped out, a witch bumped into her.

"Excuse me," said the witch. She was staring up at the ceiling. Crimson noticed that everyone was staring up—and bumping into one another.

Crimson looked up and saw why.

The ceiling was swarming with soaring brooms. Some had crooked handles. Others were long and straight. All the bristles were made of silvery straw. The straw was grown by the light of the moon. The handles were carved from lightning-struck wood. That's what gave the brooms their magic.

There were so many brooms, it seemed like the ceiling was made of them. Tags hung down on long strings so the witches could read them.

Crimson stood on her tiptoes and reached for one of the tags. "No tugging," said a saleswitch. Crimson thought she was talking to her, but then she realized the saleswitch was actually talking to a broom that she was trying to keep still. "I'll be with you in a moment," the saleswitch said to Crimson.

She had long hair that fell to her waist and bangs trimmed in a perfect line like broom bristles. Her tag read MISS WILLOW.

"Oh, I don't need a broom," said Crimson. "I'm just looking for . . ."

"A dress?" questioned Miss Willow.

"No," said Crimson. "A book on flying. Like, how to do tricks."

"Ah. Books are on the Spell Book floor," said Miss Willow. "Two floors down. The best ones on flying are published by the Spell Book Publishing House. If they don't have a book on stunts, no one does."

The Spell Book Publishing House. That was where Aunt Mildew worked. Her aunt's company hadn't published a book on Ms. Trix. "Most witches won't read about rainbow-swooping stunts," Aunt Mildew had said. Crimson had thought Broomingdale's might have more options. *I guess not,* she thought.

Crimson was about to leave when the saleswitch cried, "Twigs and toads! Not again!"

The broom Miss Willow was holding had gotten loose. It was swishing around the customers at a furious pace.

"This broom is such a bother!" said Miss Willow. "It won't hang up like the others. It's defective!"

Back and forth, back and forth it went. Unlike the other brooms, this broom had bristles that weren't straight. The bottom edge of the straw curled out like a wave.

SWISH, SWISH, SWISH.

It dusted a troll's muddy nose.

It swept the spider from a witch's hat.

It polished the warts on a wizard's toad.

It swept so hard, it left behind little sparkly rainbows.

"Stop!" cried Miss Willow.

"Stop!" squeaked the bat security.

The broom didn't stop.

Crimson knew what the problem was. She set down Pepper, whispered sternly, "Stay!" and took out her wand. She chanted:

Sweeping broom, your job is done.
Now just rest until more fun.

She said the spell again. You always have to repeat yourself for a half-size wand.

The broom stopped. It stood straight up in front of Crimson.

"Holy warts!" said Miss Willow. "How did you know to do that?"

"This is a cleaning broom, not a flying broom," explained Crimson, patting the broom on the top of its handle. "Everyone has a cleaning broom in the country. Although not one as energetic as this." She smiled. Country brooms didn't create rainbows.

"In the city we use vacuum sweepers, not cleaning

brooms," said Miss Willow. "This broom must have been shipped here by mistake. Do you want it?"

Crimson shook her head. "We already have a cleaning broom." Which she used a lot. She kept her room so clean of cobwebs, it sparkled.

"I'll have to spell it into kindling, I suppose . . ." said Miss Willow with a sigh.

"Oh, don't do that!" said Crimson. "Someone must need a cleaning broom." She had an idea. A crowd of witches crunching on frog-eye pie would leave *lots* of crumbs. "I can take it to the Moonlight Café," she said. "I'm meeting my mom there at midnight."

"Splendid!" said Miss Willow. "I'm sure some extra help there would be handy. Especially tonight." She checked her witch watch. "And it's almost midnight now."

"Already?" said Crimson. She couldn't believe it. "I haven't found anything!"

"I thought you were shopping for a book."

"Not anymore," said Crimson. "I'm not sure what I'm looking for. Unless you know of anyone who lost their . . . pet?"

Miss Willow shook her head and looked puzzled. "No. But there is a big sale on the Hat floor. Maybe you can find something there. There are lots of spectacularly spooky styles."

That sounded promising. "Thank you," said Crimson.

"No problem," said Miss Willow with a wink.

Then Crimson chanted twice to the broom:

Sweeping broom, follow me.
I'll take you where you need to be.

The broom floated beside Crimson, its bristles just grazing the floor.

"You really do know how to handle that broom," said Miss Willow. "Good luck shopping!"

Crimson smiled. She liked cleaning brooms. They were really loyal. Crimson often gave them names. Hers was called Sweepy.

"I think I'll call you Dusty," said Crimson, giving the broom another pat. She was glad to help, even if she hadn't found anything on the Broom floor. But she'd better find something soon. Miss Willow said it was almost midnight!

5

THE HAT FLOOR

Crimson pressed the elevator button shaped like a hat. She'd read about hats that were decorated in flowers. And even ones called sun hats. *Does sunshine spill out of them?* she wondered. Soon she'd find out!

Down, down, down went the elevator.

"Down, down, down," the elevator groaned. "Next it will be up, up, up. What a life."

Ding! The button shaped like a hat lit up. The elevator doors opened.

Crimson stepped out onto the Hat floor with Pepper and Dusty. In front of her were hills upon hills of hats, all stacked in perfect peaks. HALF PRICE read a sign in swirly letters.

Witches and saleswitches were rushing about, trying on hats, buying hats, and even doing demonstrations. In one corner a saleswitch had conjured a storm. Witches were standing in the rain, testing hats to ensure they were waterproof.

Crimson began to explore.

There really were lots of hats—but they all looked so similar. Extra-pointy. Pointy as scissors. Pointy as a pencil. Even "so pointy it will prick your finger," read one tag.

But there was nothing new. No flower hats. No sunshine hats. No hats that she hadn't already imagined. Broomingdale's wasn't turning out to be the store she had hoped it would be.

Then . . .

She saw, tucked in a corner, a single hat that was a little different. Well, actually it wasn't little at all. It was *huge.* And it had a bow instead of a point. The biggest, bounciest bow Crimson had ever seen! She liked it at once. And it was just the right price.

She set down the basket and Pepper hopped out. She tried on the hat. She looked at herself in a mirror. The hat was very spooky.

"What do you think?" she asked Pepper and Dusty.

Pepper yipped.

Dusty gave a swishy sweep.

They both seemed to like it.

At last, she had found something to buy.

She was just about to purchase the hat when there came a cry: "Watch out!"

Crimson pulled off the hat and looked up. Above the stack of hats a light was blinking.

And there, coming toward her, swirling and whirling, was a big black cloud.

Witches from across the floor all rushed to follow the cloud. Suddenly, Crimson got carried along with the crowd. Elbows poked. Hands grasped. Even warts were in her way as witches reached for the swirling hats.

Crimson held her breath and closed her eyes.

Whoosh!

When she opened her eyes, the cloud was gone. The big stack of hats was gone, too. All that was left was the one Crimson was holding. And some shredded scraps of fabric on the floor. Dusty happily started sweeping. *SWISH, SWISH, SWISH.*

"What was that?" asked Crimson aloud.

"A sale swarm," said a small voice beside her.

The voice belonged to a witchling.

The witchling looked about Crimson's age. She had purple eyes and purple stripes on her skirt and she was covered in bows. Bows on her shirt. Bows on her stockings. Even a bow on her wand.

"Are you going to buy that?" she asked, out of breath, pointing at the hat.

Crimson nodded.

"Oh," said the witchling. She bit her lip. "I knew it!" she said quietly. She sounded upset.

"What's wrong?" asked Crimson.

"I really like that hat. I've been saving my allowance for weeks. But that's the only one. I *told* my mom we should get here early, but she didn't listen. Then she met a friend on the roof. They kept cackling and cackling.

At last they let me come downstairs. And then, when I saw the sale swarm . . . Crowds make me feel crummy."

"There are lots of other hats," said Crimson, gesturing to the rest of the Hat floor.

"Yes," said the witchling. "But only one with a purple bow. I like bows."

"Me too," said Crimson. "But . . . not as much as you." Slowly, she handed the hat to the witchling.

"You take it," she said. "It will look better on you."

"Really?" said the witchling.

Crimson nodded.

The witchling smiled. "Thank you so much! But you are too nice. You need to learn to be more wicked."

"I know," said Crimson. "I've only just started my How-to-Be-Wicked lessons."

"Me too," said the witchling. "We must be the same age. My name is Mauve. I like your outfit."

"Thanks. My name is Crimson. This is Dusty." She pointed to the broom.

Pepper woofed.

"And that's Pepper."

Mauve crouched down and gave Pepper a pat. "He's cute. I guess you are a *little* wicked. You brought a puppy into Broomingdale's."

"Actually," said Crimson, "Pepper isn't my puppy. He's lost. Have you seen anyone looking for a lost dog?"

Mauve's purple eyes went wide. "I have!" she said. "There was a boy with his mom heading up to the Moonlight Café. I overheard him say he was looking for his puppy. His mom said that they had to stop looking, that they had to go. He seemed really upset."

"That must be Pepper's owner!" cried Crimson.

She grabbed the basket and started running across the floor, followed by Dusty.

"Wait for me," cried Mauve, who quickly paid for her hat. Then she joined Crimson and Dusty, and together they hurried to the elevator.

6

THE FASHION SHOW

Not that one. This one," said Mauve, pointing to a smaller elevator beside the main one. "This elevator takes you straight to the café."

The doors opened and they rushed inside. There was only one button, shaped like a crescent moon. Crimson pressed it. The elevator didn't say anything.

Up, up, up it went. Up to the café . . . and into the fashion show!

Broomingdale's Frightful Fashion Show was taking place in the Moonlight Café. It was busier than the broomway!

Crimson heard Mauve groan. "Wow, it's so crowded here," whispered Mauve.

"It's okay," said Crimson. "Just follow me."

Witches were wart-to-wart. And not only witches. There was a ghost wearing a bow tie. (At least Crimson thought it was a ghost. She could see only the bow tie.) And a fancy ogre so tall her head touched the ceiling. ("My poor hairdo," she fretted.) Dresses in the latest dreary shades—from gloomy green to bleakest blue—bobbed within the crowd, saying, "Buy me! Buy me!" Everyone was cackling and munching on toad toes on toast and frog-eye pie. And watching the fashion show.

All the tables had been pushed to the side, and there was a runway leading through the café out to the moonlit patio. Models strutted down it, including one of the Terribly Tasteful Triplets. Which witch, Crimson wasn't sure.

Which wizard was Pepper's owner, Crimson wasn't sure, either.

"Can you see him?" asked Crimson.

"No," said Mauve. "He must have left."

Crimson's heart sank.

She felt even worse when a cluster of witches turned their pointy noses up at her outfit, just like the teen witchlings had done earlier.

"What in the witchworld are you wearing?" exclaimed one.

"What's that on your hat?" added another.

"And *what* is going on with your toes? *Where* are the points?"

The group shook their heads in disapproval, and then, with a sniff, they turned their backs and walked away.

Crimson looked down at her outfit and felt something she'd never felt before: doubt.

In the whole store there had been only one hat with a bow. Mauve had bought that. But none of the other witches had polka dots on their dresses, and everyone, even Mauve, wore pointy black shoes. No one had boots like Crimson's.

Her thoughts were interrupted by a *SWISH!*

While she was busy with the witches, Dusty had been busy, too. Spotting crumbs.

There were lots of them littered over the floor.

SWISH, SWISH, SWISH!

The broom swept so furiously, he bumped into Crimson and she dropped the basket. Pepper leaped out.

"Oh, no!" cried Crimson.

Pepper zigzagged through the crowd. "Stop!" cried Crimson. But Pepper didn't listen.

Crimson ran after him, while Mauve stayed behind with Dusty.

"Stop, Pepper!" cried Crimson again.

But Pepper kept going.

Under the ghost's bow tie. Through the legs of the ogre. Right onto the runway.

And so did Crimson.

Poof!

It sounded like a spell. But it was actually the flash of a camera.

The crowd gasped.

Crimson gulped.

She backed up . . . into another witch on the runway.

The witch was spookily elegant, wearing a long black cape. "Witches, please excuse this frightful mista—"

But before the witch could say more, someone started to clap.

It was Mauve! Mauve—who wasn't good in crowds—was clapping and cheering as hard as she could. Soon, the rest of the crowd began to clap, too.

"Twigs and toads! How frightfully fetching!"

"How wonderfully wicked!"

"What a fashion statement!"

"Brava, Vera!"

The witch wearing the cape was the famous fashion designer Vera Fang. She looked surprised.

"What's your new line called?"

"Tell us, Vera."

Vera's mouth opened and shut like a toad catching flies.

Everyone was waiting for her to say something.

But she didn't.

Crimson looked down at her dress again. The one from Granny Twill, made just for her. "Unique like you," Granny had said. Broomingdale's didn't offer many options, even though not all witches and wizards are the same. But maybe it could. And suddenly, she knew the perfect name. "Unique," she said loudly.

Vera stood up straighter and waved her hands. "Yes, Broomingdale's Unique! For you, and you, and *you!*"

She winked at Crimson.

Crimson winked back.

Poof! Poof! Poof! More camera flashbulbs went off.

Crimson blinked. And when she opened her eyes again, she saw Pepper pounce off the stage . . . into the arms of a young wizard.

"Pepper!" cried the wizard.

7

FROG-EYE PIE

Crimson breathed a big sigh of relief. They weren't too late after all.

As Vera Fang went on about her new clothing line, Crimson slipped off the stage. She joined Pepper, his owner and the owner's mom, and Mauve and Dusty, too, near the back of the café.

Pepper's owner had messy hair. He was wearing a patchwork robe, in the same colors as Pepper's fur.

"I was so worried," said the boy, whose name was Wesley. "I thought I'd never find him."

"What happened?" asked Crimson.

"We were on the Cauldron floor when a saleswitch started giving out Beastly Biscuit samples. Pepper smelled them and jumped out of my robe pocket. I've been searching for him ever since."

The boy's mom sighed. "This wouldn't have happened if you'd left him at home, like you were supposed to."

Wesley nodded. "I know. But Pepper doesn't get

along with many witches. And I knew the mail-witch was coming. I was afraid he'd chase her. I'm surprised he didn't nip at you," he said to Crimson.

"Not once," said Crimson. "He is a really nice dog."

"He must like you," said Wesley.

Pepper barked, as if to say yes.

"Can Crimson and Mauve share some frog-eye pie with us, please, Mom?" asked Wesley. "As a reward?"

"Of course," said his mom. "It looks like the fashion show is over."

And so it was. Vera Fang had moved to the patio, where she was spelling all kinds of Unique fashions onto all the witches and wizards who wanted them.

"I feel so inspired!" she cackled, waving her wand. "That witchling is a genius."

Crimson couldn't believe it.

Or maybe she could. She smiled.

And then her stomach rumbled. "Frog-eye pie is my favorite."

"Mine too!" agreed Mauve.

So, after Crimson introduced Dusty to the chef, who was thrilled to have a cleaning broom, and Mauve said hello to her mom, who was jostling to get a one-of-a-kind cloak, they all found a table. Wesley's mom ordered them each a slice of frog-eye pie, and a big moon bone for Pepper.

The pie *was* the best thing Crimson had ever eaten. But she didn't get to eat as quickly as she wanted because Wesley and Mauve were full of questions. They had never been to Cackle County before.

"Do you go to Spell School like us?"

"Are there broom buses in the country?"

"Do you really have a next-door troll?"

"Why don't you visit?" said Crimson at last. "And you can see for yourselves. I'll have to check with my mom. But I'm sure she'll say yes."

Everyone was very excited about that.

"Where is my mom?" wondered Crimson aloud. It had to be past midnight now. Moonlight streamed through the windows of the café. "She should be here."

Crimson was just thinking of waving her wand to call her mom when, like magic, she appeared.

Her mom was in a tizzy, weighted down with bags. She didn't even seem to notice the others at the table.

"Slugs and spells! There you are, Crimson. I'm so sorry I'm late. The lines were longer than a stinkworm. And then, this fashion show! I didn't know it was taking place *here*! All these bows and polka dots . . ." She gave Crimson a funny look. "Crimson, you didn't . . ."

Crimson smiled.

Crimson's mom went wide-eyed. "Well, I suppose I'll hear all about it. Did you end up finding anything?" she added.

Suddenly, Crimson realized she hadn't. She hadn't spent a single coin. She had been planning this trip for so long, and she had nothing to show for it.

But then she paused and looked around the table.

Pepper was licking his silvery bone. Dusty was busy sweeping crumbs. Mauve and Wesley were smiling, excited about visiting Cackle County.

"Actually, I did," Crimson replied brightly. Extra brightly.

And it was true. Broomingdale's really *did* have everything a witch could itch for. Crimson had found the best thing of all. Something her gold coins couldn't buy. Friends.